Back to the Farm with Darla - A Sexy Sequel

Dirk Caldwell Romantic Erotic Novels, Volume 9

Dirk Caldwell

Published by Dirk Caldwell, 2023.

BACK TO THE FARM WITH DARLA - A SEXY SEQUEL

First edition. September 12, 2023.

Copyright © 2023 Dirk Caldwell.

ISBN: 979-8223307310

Written by Dirk Caldwell.

Also by Dirk Caldwell

Dirk Caldwell Romantic Erotic Novels
A Visit to the Farm with Darla - a Sexy Short Story
A Layover in Omaha with Tina
A Night in Eufaula with Lynn
A Trip to the Lake with Kim
Older Women need Love, too! Erika visits Atlanta
Lessons in Love: Gabriella visits Indianapolis
Big Girls Need Love, too! Barbara from Kokomo
Flight Attendants want Love: Flying High with Jessica
Back to the Farm with Darla - A Sexy Sequel

Table of Contents

Acknowledgment

Cover image by Freepik
Back Cover generic airline pilot image by Blake Guidry at unsplash

Introduction

My name is Dirk. Well, that's not my real name. I'd never be able to have a normal life if I used my real name. I was an enlisted guy in the Air Force and single at the start of this encounter. I enjoyed being unencumbered and the benefits that came from that. I could travel the world as an international aircrew member and be with any woman I wanted without regret and have always enjoyed the freedom that came with that ability.

I love women. I like them all, tall, short, fat, thin, old, or young. Attractive women and not-so-attractive are all the same to me. I specialize in dating women who are not getting enough attention due to their shape, size, appearance, age, or whatever. There are a lot of women that are underserved in that category. One of the few limits I put on choosing women was a lower age limit of 21, I'm no child molester. I had not experienced an upper limit as yet but have had sex with some ladies that were in their 50s and 60s that were a great lay. Most of the women in the unappreciated and underserved category I had sex with the most were horny as hell due to lack of attention and their behavior in bed showed that. Each woman was different, and I wanted to sample as many of them as possible before getting tied down. If I ever do get tied down.

I noticed that some women and I had a powerful sexual attraction for some reason. Maybe it was that they intuitively knew I would give them the attention they yearned for. I'm not sure why it happened, for some reason some women get very aggressive when it comes to sex, and many wanted to try new things. I was happy to help. I have a lot of repeat customers, and just as many that wanted sex once and were satisfied with that. Even after giving my usual disclaimer that I am not looking for a long-term relationship, I've had some close calls.

I enjoy recalling some of my favorite encounters. Most were great, some were just okay, and some I absolutely could not believe what happened. These are the encounters I write about, as they are the most entertaining and fun to read about. While most of the content in my stories is true, I do spice things up every now and then, but you would be surprised how much happened exactly as written. I've been incredibly lucky with women and am humbled every day that I have had so much success.

As a disclaimer, I always change enough of the information about the ladies so my writing could not possibly be traced back to them. Cities are changed, along with names, occupations, specific characteristics, branches of service for the military, etc. To do otherwise would not be gentlemanly. I do, however, mix in some of my local knowledge about locations. How did I get that information? Let your imagination be your guide.

I hope you enjoy my novels.

Saturday on the Farm

I got a call from my friend Darla, with whom I had a wild experience at her place a while ago. She had some work that needed a strong back and asked for help on a certain Saturday. I had the weekend off from Air Force duty, so I agreed to meet her at her farm at a certain time. I was a single senior enlisted guy at the time, in a management position and usually worked office hours unless I was on a trip. Thinking of the exciting time I had with Darla on my last visit, I was looking forward to my second trip to the farm.

Near the appointed hour, I rolled up to the farm and parked next to her house. I looked around for her as I did the first time, finally locating her out at the barn a couple of hundred feet from the house. Darla was in a small building that stored horse feed, saddles, and supplies and was busy moving some stuff around.

After greeting her and giving her a quick kiss that she did not seem too interested in, she explained that she was cleaning up old feed bags and trash in preparation for a trip to the feed store for more feed. Darla was dressed in a snug purple tank top with no bra, which accentuated her nice medium boobs. She was also wearing a navy golf skirt, which looked nice with her sturdy tanned legs. Her long dark hair was pulled back into a simple ponytail, and she had mud shoes on her feet. She wore a watch but no other jewelry and looked the part of a horsewoman working at the barn.

It was still summer in Louisiana, and with the humidity, I was sweating already, and I had not started working yet. I started hauling empty feed sacks out to her one-ton dually truck, which was parked next to the building we were working at. After getting dozens of empty sacks stowed in the truck and some other trash loaded, she announced we were ready to head south to the town of Benton for the trip to the feed store. We would make a stop by some parish (county) community dumpsters on the way to get rid of the trash, then hit the feed store. After coming back to the barn with the feed, we would stack the feed sacks and then be done with our chores. I hoped there would be some time for sex in there somewhere, but it did not sound like it at this point. What the hell, I had plenty of sex the last time I was here, maybe this time I was just going to be a good friend and provide grunt work. I wiped the sweat from my brow and headed for the truck.

To my surprise, she wanted me to drive the truck. I did not mind, so we got in, and after adjusting the mirrors I carefully pulled out and headed to Benton. She pointed out the dumpsters, and we stopped to unload the trash. After that, we were on Louisiana Highway 3 heading into Benton, when Darla moved her legs up onto the bench seat towards me and said something, so I looked over at her. She had pulled up her tank top to expose her boobs, which I had seen before but was glad to see again. She also had hiked up her skirt to show that she had no panties on, and I had a clear look at her shaved pussy. I damned near drove off the side of the road.

Grinning, she said, "I thought I'd give you a look to see what you will be getting later."

"I appreciate that! Will there be a later?"

"For sure! After we get our work done, that is. I'm horny as hell and have some things I want to do with you. You can think about that while we are working."

"That will definitely have me thinking."

I had seen the feed store on the way north from the air base and pulled in when we got to Benton. Darla went in to negotiate the feed purchase, and after a while to let my boner subside, I joined her and had a nice visit with the feed store folks. Since this was my first visit, I got a free feed store hat, which became one of my prized possessions. The feed store dudes started loading bags of feed onto the truck, and when I thought they were done, went back for another load. I asked, "How much did she buy?"

The answer was, "A ton of feed, and some other grains."

I thought for a minute. A ton of feed? At 50 pounds per bag, that was 40 sacks plus whatever supplements she had ordered. Holy crap, that's a lot of feed. My back was thinking about aching already. Darla hopped back into the truck and announced we were ready to head back to the farm.

It's Fun to get Feed

I pulled out with the maximum load on the back of the truck, and it wasn't a mile or so out of town when Darla took her seat belt off, slid over, and lay on her back, putting her head on my lap, facing up towards me. Looking down, I saw her smiling.

"This is one of the things I have a fantasy about. Driving in my truck with someone playing with me. Give me your hand."

I moved my hand to hers, and she first placed it on her boobs, which were once again in view. I played with them for a while and tried to keep the truck between the lines as I snuck a peek now and then. Thank goodness for cruise control, it reduced the workload. Her boobs were nice, I enjoyed that a lot. Then she took my hand and placed it on her naked shaved pussy under the golf skirt. I played with her labia for a while, then she pulled my hand in tighter, so I slid a finger into her pussy. She moaned a little, and as I massaged her G spot, her hips started moving and she became more agitated. I almost missed the turn off the highway but made it at the last minute with heavy braking and one hand turning the wheel.

I played with her pussy as I drove, with a lot of moaning and squirming. As I massaged her G spot for a few more minutes and then tickled her clit, her moaning became louder and more intense. She braced her feet against the passenger side door window with her legs spread as far as she could get them, one in the front corner of the window and one at the back corner. I noticed she had shed her work shoes and I saw her sock clad feet. With a mile or so to go to her driveway, she could wait no longer and began crying out.

"Oh, God! I'm about to come! Oh, yeah! Oh! Oh! Ahhhhhh!!"

With her feet on the passenger window and her head in my lap, she arched her back and raised her hips off the bench seat, bucking into my hand. It was very hard to stay on the road.

"Uhhhhhhhhhh! Ahhhhhh! Oh, God! Oh! Oh! Oh, shit! Oh, shit!"

Her hips collapsed back onto the seat and her feet came down from the window as her orgasm passed. I kept up a gentle pressure on her clit as she lay still, breathing heavily. I looked down and saw her eyes closed with a smile on her face.

I braked for her driveway, and retrieved my wet right hand from her pussy to help turn in. She raised up and pointed out where the truck should go. As I pulled the truck into position by the barn, she got out and went back to the tail gate and lowered it. She indicated I should sit on the tail gate, so I did.

Darla then unzipped my shorts, deftly pulled out my erect cock, and began an enthusiastic blow job, which was much appreciated. After a few minutes of that pleasurable activity, she rose and asked me to pull a feed sack down from the pile. She climbed up on the sack and lay on her back on top of it, then lifted her golf skirt, exposing her shiny wet pussy. With me standing at the tailgate, she was at the perfect fucking height. My cock was still wet from her saliva and extended from my shorts. She grabbed it and pulled me to her and guided me into her.

I got the idea and pushed into her, with her groaning in appreciation as I hit the bottom of the vaginal vault and made contact with her cervix. I started an enthusiastic thrusting motion and was rewarded by her hips pushing into me as she matched each thrust. This was incredible! I was fucking Darla on top of a feed sack on the tailgate of a truck out in the open. This must have been one of her fantasies. If she had any more, I'd be glad to participate.

With the sun beating down on us as we sweated and pushed into each other, we became hotter sexually and physically as I pounded into her, loving her tight, wet pussy and the enthusiasm.

She cried out, "Harder! Harder!" so I started really drilling her. I lifted her legs and got even deeper, and she groaned with pleasure.

"My pussy is still tingling! Do it harder!"

Within a few minutes of heavy fucking, I was near orgasm.

I called out, "I'm about to come!"

She cried out, "Pull out!"

I pulled my dick out and she guided my cock to her belly, where she pumped it a few times, then it exploded in cum all over her stomach and hairless pubic area. I closed my eyes and groaned loudly as I ejaculated in several spurts, while she pumped my cock with her fist. It felt great, though I was wondering why she did not want me to come inside her. She filled me in almost immediately.

"I want you to eat my pussy later, so I needed to keep it clean. Sorry, I just thought of that."

"No problem. Glad we made it work."

She asked me to get a towel out of the barn, and we mopped up the cum on her belly. She sat up and pulled her top down and arranged her skirt. "Whew! That's the way to go to the feed store! Let's get these sacks unloaded."

Since I was still fully dressed, I was hotter than shit and soaked in sweat. We walked to the house and hit the restroom, then got a drink. We walked back and started unloading the 40 freaking bags of feed, stacked just right so they would not fall over. After getting a ton of feed straightened out, my back was tired, so I watched her do horse chores for a while until the next event.

After tending other horses and cleaning the barn stalls for about an hour, Darla got a huge grey horse out of his stall and led him to a sturdy post next to the barn. She then started brushing him and generally getting him ready to ride, during which I assumed I would be a spectator. She saddled the beast with an English style saddle, then looked at me and said, "I'll let these stirrups way out, your legs are pretty long."

I asked, "Why do you need to do that? Aren't you going to ride him?"

She grinned. "You are going to be the one in the saddle, and I'll ride you."

I began to understand. "Oh, another one of your fantasies?"

She smiled shyly. "Something like that."

"You'll have to explain that to me."

"I'll do better than that, I'll show you. Come in the barn with me."

Leaving the big horse tied to the pole, she led me into the barn to the stack of feed sacks. She climbed up on one of the stacks, turned towards me, and spread her legs with a big smile on her face.

"I've been thinking about you doing some magic on my pussy with your tongue. Are you up for that?"

I was indeed. "Sure thing, and you are at the perfect height. Lift your skirt and show me what you have."

She slowly and provocatively lifted the golf skirt so her pussy was in view. It was a thing of beauty, with freshly shaved skin and a small tuft of black curls over her clit that I remember admiring on our first encounter. It was very inviting.

"Nice, now show me the boobs."

She kept the smile on her face and lifted the tank top until her boobs came out, bouncing a little as they came free of the top. Her boobs were a nice size, probably a 34B, with erect pink nipples.

I was ready to move in but had a question. "What about the horse?"

"He'll be all right there for a few minutes while you get me all riled up. C'mon! Get started!"

I wanted to slow down her aggressive style a little. "Spread your pussy lips."

She grinned again and squirmed her hips a little. Her hand went to her pussy and with two fingers, she spread the labia. It looked luscious and pink. I bent over and gave her a lick between the lips, right in the pink. It smelled wonderful, aromatic with sweat, the classic aroma of anchovy scented cunt, and the previous fuck. She moaned and her hips moved.

I then went north, licking the inside of the lips as I went, ending up at the clitoris with the small patch of hair. I gave that a tickle, which got a moan in response. Back south I went, enjoying the sights of the shaved pussy and the scents, wet with pussy juice and my saliva. I ended up at the hole leading to the vaginal vault, which I entered and shoved my tongue in deeply, then curving it up to get at the G spot. She gasped and moaned, then cried out.

"Damn! That's perfect! How in the world did you learn how to do that?"

I pulled back and smiled at her. "I had lessons from an Italian sexpot."

She gasped, "You were paying attention in class. Do it a little more, then we'll mount up."

I gave her several more licks up and down and in and out to increasingly loud moans, and then I stood up.

"Get in front of me. I want some more of that pussy before we do it on the horse."

She climbed down and bent over in front of me. I slipped my rock hard cock into her and gave some hard thrusts into her wet and tight hole.

"Damn, Darla! That is some damned fine pussy! I love it!"

She laughed as I pounded into her. "I remember that you liked it this way!"

I pulled out after a minute of very pleasurable fucking. "What's next on the fantasy agenda?"

"Let's go out and get on Blue."

I was puzzled. "What's a Blue?"

"The horse's name is Blue. He's a thoroughbred gelding, unlike you. You're a stud."

Riding Blue

We walked out to the massive horse who was waiting patiently. She had me approach Blue from the left side, and standing on a mounting block, I followed her directions and put my left foot into the stirrup, and then swung aboard, all with my erect cock hanging out. I was way up in the air in the saddle with both feet in the stirrups with my cock protruding in front of me. "What's next?"

She was grinning. "Now I mount you!"

She then got up on the mounting block, and with me lifting her left leg that came close to kicking me in the face, got her in front of me, facing me. We were very close together, in sweaty contact with our entire torsos, her legs straddling mine. Her pussy was in hard contact with my cock.

She then said, "Lift me up, and I'll slip your dick in me."

I put my hands on her waist and lifted her as she took my cock in one hand while she braced herself on me with the other, and soon my dick was sliding into her very wet pussy as she faced me.

I was astounded by the feeling. "Damn! This is great!"

She moaned and smiled as she felt my dick go all the way in her. She then reached around behind her and unclipped Blue from the post, while handing me the reins.

"Pull back on the reins a little and push your heels in at the same time."

I did so and was amazed that Blue backed away from the post.

She gasped, "Now pull the reins a little to the right and tap your heels gently into his side."

Big Blue turned to the right and started walking. Darla gasped in pleasure at the feeling of the horse bouncing along with my dick buried in her.

"Oh, shit! That feels better than I had hoped for. Every time he takes a step, your dick pushes hard into me, and my clit gets a push. Damn, that feels good! Lead him to the gate that's open and he'll go through on his own."

I did so and Blue turned into the pasture on his own, walking with a steady gait.

I felt fantastic, with Darla impaled on my dick with her arms around my neck. She moaned as the horse moved, and I pumped into her in the same rhythm. For the first time, she pulled my face to hers and kissed me deeply and passionately. Then she cried out.

"Ahh, that is so damned good. Keep pumping into me! My pussy is tingling!"

I kept up my pumping and started caressing her boobs and nipples to keep things hot as we walked for a few minutes.

She gasped again. "Okay! Now kick your heels into him a little and make a clucking sound, he'll start trotting."

I was looking forward to this. I kicked my heels gently into Blue and made a clucking sound. He knew what to do. We started trotting.

Darla was losing her mind with the different motion.

"Ahhhhhh! Oh, damn. Oh, shit. Oh, that feels good. Keep pumping me!"

I had no problem with that. She grabbed my face and again kissed me deeply and her moans increased.

"Oh! Ahhhh! Errrrrahhh! Oh, damn! I'm coming! I'm coming! Oh, shit! Ahhhhhh!"

As big Blue trotted happily around the field, we ground our hips against each other and pumped frantically, each achieving orgasm at almost the same time. I groaned loudly as my cock pumped load after load of cum deep into Darla.

She collapsed against me, and I pulled the reins back a little. Blue slowed to a walk and then stopped, wondering what we wanted next. After a moment, she looked around and instructed, "Move your reins to one side towards the barn. He'll know to go there."

I did, and Blue turned to the barn at a slow walk. I looked into Darla's face, so close to mine.

"How arc you doing, honey?"

She smiled at me. "Fantastic! That fulfills another fantasy. Only two or three to go!"

I laughed. "I'm not sure I can handle another. That was great!"

She laughed and kissed me again while my cock was still in her as we bounced along as Blue walked back to the barn, with cum and pussy juice leaking out of her onto our thighs and her saddle. "We're a mess!"

"Yeah, but it was fun!"

Blue walked up to the post and stood there calmly. Darla reached around behind her and managed to clip the rope to Blue's halter, in case he decided to go elsewhere. Coordinating with her, I lifted her by her waist until my cock came out, then helped her swing a leg around until she had both feet on one side of the horse, then she nimbly jumped to the ground. She pulled the mounting block closer and helped me get my leg over the big horse and onto solid ground. I patted Blue affectionally on the neck. The saddle was a mess. She went to the barn and got another two towels, one for the saddle and the other for the goo running down her thighs and my wet cock.

We stood there toweling off as the big horse looked at us curiously. She was the first to comment.

"Holy crap, that was great! That's the most intense feeling I've ever had. There was so much pressure on my pussy it was unbelievable! And that pounding went straight into me when Blue started trotting! Wow. Your dick was so deep in me I thought it would rupture me."

"I loved it, but are you hurt at all?"

"I can tell I'll be sore tomorrow, but it's a good kind of hurt. Shit, we need to take care of Blue. Help me get his saddle off and I'll brush him down."

Darla unhooked the saddle and pulled it off. I put it on a rack in the barn after trying to wipe off the wetness. She then brushed Blue down and led him to his stall, then decided it was close enough to horsey dinnertime to feed the herd. I watched as she opened feed sacks and mixed some supplements into buckets, then added the feed. I helped carry the feed to the stalls and fill water buckets. With that finished, we walked back to the house, sticky with sex fluids, sweat, and dust from cleaning out stalls.

Evening fun

After drinking some water, we got into the shower together as we had done during my last visit. It was great fun to soap each other off. I especially liked doing her boobs and pussy from behind her. She held up her hair for me to wash her back, which was intimate and tender. My cock got a little stiff when she washed it, but I was too fucked out to pursue anything.

Afterward, she wanted to plan the evening while we were toweling off.

"Can you stay for a while, or even the night?"

"Sure, I'm wide open."

She smiled. "Good, I got some stuff to drink and some heavy snacks. Will that be okay for dinner?"

I nodded. "Drinks and snacks are what we aircrew members thrive on. Let's get started with drinks."

We got dressed, sort of. She put on a long tee shirt and that was it. I wasn't complaining. I had thought ahead and had an overnight bag in the car, so I put on clean shorts and a tee shirt.

In the large farm-style kitchen, she showed me what she had bought. "I got you Jim Beam and Diet Pepsi; I thought you liked those. I'll have the same."

I smiled. "That's perfect!"

She got me some glassware and I mixed drinks for us while she got out some snacks. We went into the living room and sat together on a loveseat. She turned on the TV and we watched the local news. The weather report was for hot and humid conditions, with a chance for evening thunderstorms. I wasn't missing anything by staying the night, but thought I had better check.

"Darla? Just making sure, did you want me to spend the night? I'd love to, but don't want to impose."

She smiled at me, saying, "I'd like for you to stay. I haven't had a man stay for the night in a long time. You're kind of special."

It was my turn to smile. "In that case, I can have another drink or two."

She nodded. "Me, too. I still have several fantasies that you need to help me with."

"Oh? What are they?"

She smiled coyly. "I need to get a little drunk before I tell you."

I was intrigued. "I'm fascinated. Let me know when the time is right. In the meantime, it's a good time to remind each other that we are friends with benefits and not looking for a serious commitment."

She nodded enthusiastically. "I'm fully on board with that. I like you a lot, and enjoy having crazy hot sex with you, but really don't want a man around all the time."

I felt a sense of relief. "Thanks, Darla. We are on the same wavelength. I like acting like boyfriend and girlfriend when we are together if that's all right with you."

She smiled shyly. "I kind of like that with you."

I put my arm around her and leaned in for a kiss. She responded well, and after that, we held hands in affectionate silence and watched some game shows after the news was over. We finished another drink, and I was glad I was staying the night. I didn't want to risk a career-ending DUI like many of my colleagues had. I got up to use the restroom, but she stopped me.

"Are you heading to the bathroom to pee?"

I was a little tipsy. "Why yes, I am. Did you want to watch or help?"

She giggled. "It's time for another fantasy. Come outside with me."

"But I really have to pee!"

She took me by the hand. "Even better. Come on!"

We walked out into the early evening darkness to the fence line of the horse pasture. There she announced her fantasy.

"I've always wanted to hold a man's dick while they pee, spraying it all around and maybe make a design. Will you let me do that?"

In my semi-drunken state, I could not think of a downside. "Sure! Why not!"

I unzipped my shorts and pulled my limp dick out. She took ahold of it with one hand and said, "Go ahead!"

This was a little unusual, so it took a minute for me to convince my bladder to have urine start flowing. Once used to the idea, a steady stream came out, and she giggled and laughed as she directed the stream here and there until my bladder was empty. With a few dribbles stubbornly cling to the tip of the penis, I told her to shake it gently. A drop of urine got on her hand.

"Rookie mistake! Now you need to wash your hands, which of course you should do anyway."

She said, "Thanks! That fantasy has been fulfilled."

"Tell me about the others."

She laughed as we walked back into the house. "I'm still not drunk enough yet."

"In that case, let's have another drink!"

After washing our hands, we met in the kitchen, where I mixed a strong drink for each of us. We both took a swallow, after which she said, "Wow! This ought to do it!"

"I'm curious, and I want to get to satisfying your fantasies. By the way, it's been a while since I played with your boobs." I reached up under her shirt and gave the bare boobs some love and kissed her deeply while doing so. As I reached under her shirt, it lifted and exposed her bare ass, so I caressed that, too.

She smiled as we came up for air. "This boyfriend/girlfriend stuff is kind of fun, like its own fantasy. Getting drunk helps!"

"I aim to please, dear girl."

"So, the boyfriend fantasy is that we'll be in love for the weekend, then I'll dump you. We'll be broken up until I need you to screw me again, at which point I will call you and you will be grateful."

I laughed. "Will I come crawling back to you and beg for your womanly charms?"

She grinned. "That works. Are you just going to stand there feeling me up, or do you want to go back to the couch?"

I gave her nipples a last little squeeze. "To the couch!"

She kissed me while giggling. "You're so crazy."

We sat on the couch and tried to concentrate on a movie as she curled up into me with my arm around her, but being a bit drunk and with the knowledge that she was naked under the tee shirt, it was hard to focus. She had a hand on my thigh, and every now and then gave my cock a friendly stroke on the outside of my shorts. I ran my hand up her naked thigh a few times to show that I was still interested, stopping short of her pussy but getting very close.

After a long while of this subtle foreplay, I said the hell with it and pulled her onto my lap, with her legs across me. I had good access to her legs, pussy, and boobs which was all I was interested in at this point. We kissed long and deeply as our hands roamed each other. I ran my fingers over her labia, which made her gasp with excitement. After several very enjoyable minutes of this, she sat up and tugged my shirt up and over my head, so my torso was naked. Then she pulled her shirt off and was now totally naked on my lap. That made exploration easier, so I upped the ante by cupping her boobs in my hands and kissing the nipples, giving them a little teasing bite along the way.

She sat against me with a smile on her face and her eyes closed, relishing the attention. Her hands moved over my bare chest as I returned the favor. I put a hand down to her pussy, and she spread her legs to make it easier on me. My fingers played with her labia, and then made an initial visit to the hole of her vaginal vault. She groaned and her hips moved as I tickled her G spot from within. Her eyes opened, and then she bent down to kiss and nibble at my nipples, which I thought was incredibly erotic.

After a minute, she said, "I can tell by how hard your cock is that you like that."

"It is telling the truth. I like that a lot."

She then leaned her face next to mine and nibbled my ear lobe and then whispered in my ear. "Want to go to the bedroom?"

"What's wrong with the couch?"

She smiled seductively. "I need something from the bedroom."

We stood up and drained our drinks, both fairly drunk but able to walk. She turned off the TV and the light, and we staggered down the long hallway to the master bedroom. She looked over her shoulder at me walking behind her.

"Are you watching my ass?"

"I've not taken my eyes off your magnificent buttocks."

She laughed and gave it an exaggerated wiggle, which was nice to watch. She really did have a nicely shaped ass.

We arrived at the bedroom, where she turned to me. "Stand here by my side of the bed and slip your shorts off."

She lay on the bed and watched me intently, smiling as my rock-hard cock popped out and bobbed.

"Now parade around the bed like a stripper and show off your boner."

I was drunk enough not to feel self-conscious, so I gave her my best male stripper imitation as I walked around the bed a few times, stopping to pose and even managed to wiggle my hips which made my erect dick wiggle and bob. She giggled and clapped.

"That was great! I've always wanted a man to do that for me. Thanks! Now we'll get to the last fantasy."

Back Door Fantasy Fulfilled

She reached into the bedside table and pulled out a couple of washcloths and a small jar of Vaseline.

She patted the bed next to her. I sat down, and she handed me the jar of Vaseline. "Now grease me up and fuck me in the ass!"

I was mildly surprised, but eager to help. "Is this one of the fantasies?"

She nodded and grinned. "Yeah, I've never done this before. I wanted to lose my ass cherry with you. Will it hurt?"

"You'll feel some intense sensation as I enter your anal sphincter, then that will subside a bit. I'll ease it in a little at a time, and if you tell me to stop or pull out, and I'll do that right away."

She was staring into my eyes, then nodded. "I trust you, Dirk. I'll do whatever you say. How do you want me?"

"I'll keep playing with you until you are pretty wound up, then fuck your pussy for a while to get us both more worked up. Then I'll have you roll over doggie style, that lets me control the penetration better. It can be done facing each other, too but for this first time I want to be ready to pull out quickly if you need me to."

She grinned as she stroked my very hard cock. "You're wound up enough. You just want back in my pussy!"

"I'm not going to lie, that is a major factor."

I lay next to her and played with her boobs and nipples as I ran a finger up and down her labia, poking into the vaginal vault every now and then and giving the G spot a tickle. After a few minutes of this very pleasant activity, her hips began squirming against me.

"Put it in me, Dirk! I'm hot enough!"

I placed the head of my rock-hard cock against her lips and pushed in gently, with her sighing in bliss as it made its way to the bottom of her vagina.

"Just fuck me slow for a couple of minutes."

I did, and she moaned as we enjoyed getting hotter and hotter.

She then whispered into my ear, "Put it in my ass."

I had her roll over to the doggie style position and took the tin of Vaseline and applied a gob of it on her anus, then gently worked it in with my finger. She moaned a little as my finger entered her asshole. I then greased up my cock, and with another gob of the jelly on the purple knob of my dick, placed it against her asshole. She braced herself on hands and knees, totally giving herself to me.

I asked, "Ready?"

"Yes. Do it!"

"It may hurt a little as the anus gets stretched out, then it will be pressure and some intense feeling."

"Okay. I trust you. I can feel you pushing on my asshole. Give it to me!"

I pushed against the initial resistance of the anus until my glans got on the other side of the sphincter, then waited for a reaction.

She had one. "Ohh, that is fucking crazy! Can you wait a minute?"

"Yeah, I'm going to go a little bit at a time, then wait until you tell me to stop, or I'll keep going until I'm all the way in."

After a minute, she said, "It's better now. You were right about the stretching. Wow, that is intense."

"Okay, here is some more." I eased in another inch or two and waited again.

She said, "Oh. That's a lot. Stay there a minute. I can't believe I am having you do this to me."

I waited and caressed her ass and boobs for something to do.

"A little more. Wow. That's some kind of feeling."

I pushed in a little more. "I can start in and out a little, so you can see what that's like."

"Yeah, go ahead."

I started a gentle back and forth pumping.

"You can go deeper, it's feeling better."

"Here we go." I pushed in a little more and waited for feedback.

She gasped, "That's not too bad. Keep going."

I gave her boobs some attention and gave her clit a little tickle for good measure. I pushed in a little more, being careful not to overwhelm her. A few minutes later of slow progress, I announced, "I'm all the way in."

She was shocked. "So, your cock is all the way up my ass?" She took a moment to visualize the length of my shaft up inside her. "No shit. Okay, fuck me real slow."

I started a gentle in-and-out thrusting, enjoying the squeeze of her around my swollen dick. I checked on how she was doing. "How's that feeling?"

"It's amazing! Do a lot of your girlfriends like this?"

I had to chuckle. "For a few women I know, that's all they want to do."

"Mmmm. I can see why."

I fucked her a little faster, to the accompaniment of some good moaning. She was getting hotter. Some women will come during anal sex, some don't. I had a feeling Darla would.

Her head raised up, and she moaned loudly, then said, "I'm getting really tingly in my pussy. Do women come during this?"

"Some do."

"Damn! Go deeper and faster!"

I complied and was banging away pretty fast.

"Are you going to come?"

"I'd say very soon. This is really tight."

"You can go faster if you need to come but play with my clit!"

I pumped a little faster, and in a few minutes felt my balls load up for another salvo. I gasped, "I'm about to come!"

She cried out, "Squeeze my boobs! Rub my clit! Oh, shit! Oh, shit! What the fuck? I'm going to come with you in my ass! Ahhhhhhh! Oh, no! Oh, wow!"

She threw her head back and let out a low scream.

"AAAAHHHHHHH! Oh, my god! Oh, shit! Fuck! Damn! Owwwwww!"

I couldn't take it anymore, and cut loose with a salvo of cum into her tight asshole.

She pushed her ass back into me and wiggled it back and forth for added enjoyment as her orgasm passed over her. Then she collapsed onto the bed. I fell onto her back as the room spun around me, a combination of the booze and sensation from a great ass fuck. After a moment, I raised up and caressed her ass and back.

"How are you doing, Darla?"

She raised up on her elbows and looked around at me with a grin. "That was fucking great! I've never felt anything like that!"

I could see she was a convert for anal sex. Some women love it, others tolerate it, and others hate it after trying it once.

I pulled out of her ass with a plop, and took a moment to admire a trail of cum leaking out of the anus. I wiped it gently with a washcloth, then she reached back and took the cloth it and stuffed it between her ass cheeks. She rolled over, shook her head again, grinned, then ran for the bathroom.

I used the time to wipe my dick off and lay back on the bed catching my breath. She came out a few minutes later, and lay next to me. I put my arm around her as she snuggled up. Ever practical, she said, "Wash your dick off before you pull the sheets up. They're new."

"Yes, dear."

She giggled. "That sounded like a housewife, didn't it? I let you fuck me in my ass but you better not get my sheets stained! That's not me, really."

I kissed her. "I'll go wash up now." I headed to the bathroom and gave my limp cock a nice wash with warm water and soap, then returned to the bed.

She was looking at me. "What now?"

I pondered the possibilities. "We could go to sleep. We could also go get another drink, have a snack and watch some more TV. Or, we could gaze into each other's eyes and say sweet romantic things to each other."

"I vote for a drink and snack, and the late show."

"Let's do it."

I made us another drink as she got out some more snacks. We settled back onto the loveseat, with her wearing the same tee shirt, but this time with a wad of tissue between her butt cheeks to catch any leakage. I put my shorts and shirt back on and we snuggled as we watched the late night TV comic do his thing.

As that show ended, she looked up at me and said, "That was fantastic. I want you to do that to me every time you visit me."

"So, you want me to visit you again? Haven't you run out of fantasies?"

"Of course, I want you to visit me, jerk! Just not every weekend." She couldn't help laughing as she said it.

I tried to look offended. "I'm crushed!"

She tucked herself into me and put a hand on my face. "Don't worry, you'll get plenty of chances to visit. Do you live on the air base?"

"No, I have an house in Shreveport."

She looked into my eyes. "Maybe I could come visit you there sometimes. We could even go on a real date."

"What, coming to see you on the farm is not a real date?"

She had a good laugh. "It seems that all we do is fuck here on the farm."

I protested, "No, you make me do manual labor, too!"

"Well, you have me there. We could go out to eat, maybe go to a movie or something."

I tried to pout. "You'd just break up with me after using me."

"Yeah, that's the idea. I use you for sex, you use me for sex, we have a few laughs and go our own way until the next time."

I kissed her. "Sounds like a plan."

She yawned and stretched. "Let's go to bed."

We climbed into bed, with one strange event. As I was in the bathroom brushing my teeth, she came in naked then sat on the commode next to the sink I was using and peed. I looked at her as she was urinating, she did not bat an eye. Odd.

We snuggled for a minute, then she laid some ground rules. "I don't mind snuggling for a minute, but after that, I don't like to be touched while I sleep."

"Fair enough. Good night." She was not a real touchy-feely person, except on her terms. I rolled away from her after a minute, and as I went to sleep, thought about this visit to the farm. It was full of new experiences and was exceptional.

Morning on the Farm

When I woke up, I was alone in the bed. After using the restroom and getting dressed, I looked around the big farmhouse for Darla but, did not find her. I looked out the window and saw her at the barn, doing horse stuff, I presumed. There was some coffee made in the kitchen, with a clean mug next to the pot. I poured myself a cup and had a few swallows, then felt guilty about her working at the barn by herself. I went out the back door with my coffee and walked to the barn.

She noticed me and said hello. "Glad to see you made it out of bed. I thought you military guys were early risers."

"Not this guy. What are you up to?"

"The usual barn shit I do every morning. Can you fill the water buckets?"

I filled the buckets as the morning sun warmed up the humid Louisiana day.

"It's already getting hot."

She nodded. "This time of year, it pays to get the chores done early."

Finishing up after a few minutes of activity, she brushed her hands on a towel. Darla was wearing another tight tank top, showing her nice boobs in profile as the morning light illuminated her from the side. She was wearing shorts and her work shoes and had her hair pulled back into the usual ponytail. She wore a visor and sunglasses against the glare of the sun.

She looked over at me. "Well, now that we have talked about the weather and gotten the chores done, the question is do you want to have morning sex here in the barn, or in the bedroom?"

I was not ready for that question. "What's your preference?"

She looked thoughtful. "Here in the barn on the feed sacks was kind of kinky, almost like one of my fantasies. Yeah, let's do it out here. I'm already a little sweaty, do you mind?"

I wanted to be gallant. "Not at all. After you." My cock was waking up with all the sexy talk.

We entered the barn, and after she removed the sunglasses and visor, she pulled the tank top off over her head, revealing her nice boobs. She then came to me and pulled my shirt off and we stood there with only our shorts on. She had me move a couple of feed sacks so that she would be at my waist level, then reached up to a shelf for something, then lay back onto her elbows with a grin.

"You can do my shorts if you want to."

"I'm happy to help undress you!"

As she cooperatively raised her hips, I pulled her shorts down to her ankles and pulled her shoes off to facilitate removing them all the way, noting there were no panties. Clad in only her socks, she lay on the feed sacks with her legs spread, looking at me, still grinning.

"You have too many clothes on."

"I'll take care of that right now!" I quickly removed my shorts and shoes, and like her was naked except for my socks. The barn was already hot, and the Louisiana humidity was causing us to sweat even before we exerted ourselves.

She provocatively rubbed her pussy with a free hand. "I'd like some head, then I'll let you fuck my pussy for a while before you fuck my ass. Here's some Vaseline." She handed me a jar of the stuff.

My eyebrows went up. "Oh, so that's the plan? When do I get my dick sucked?"

Thinking for a brief moment, she said, "How about right now?" she then rolled onto her back and said, "Put it in my mouth, then you can throat fuck me for a while."

"Throat fuck? What's that?"

She laughed. "I'll show you."

Darla then laid her head way back facing up, assuming a sword swallower position, and guided my rigid cock into her mouth. With some hip motion, I was in her throat as her tongue circled my shaft. I moved in and out a little, with her handling it well. Then she reached behind me and grabbed my ass and pulled me deeper into her throat. I pushed in a little, enjoying the feeling. I stopped deep in her throat and felt her swallow. It felt incredible. I moved in and out a little more, then pulled out. She rolled over with a grin while saliva dripped from her mouth.

Wiping the drool away with the back of her hand, she asked, "What did you think about that?"

"Damn, Darla! That was fucking incredible! How in the world did you learn that?"

She laughed. "I've been practicing on zucchini. I wanted to be able deep throat you now and not gag. Are you surprised?"

I was amazed. "Hell yes. I'd like a full blow job like that sometime!"

"You got it. Now give me some head before I explode!"

I moved my head between her legs and commenced to go into her labia, licking up and down, stopping at the clit for a lick on the north side, and delving into her hole on the southbound leg. I curled my tongue into her G spot and felt her squirm and heard her moan. She was getting hotter by the second. Her slick pussy was fantastic, and I reveled in the aroma of hot cunt as I concentrated my efforts on the G spot and felt and heard her writhing with desire.

After several minutes of intense pussy licking, she was begging me to fuck her.

"C'mon, Dirk. Put it in me! I want it bad! Please!"

I stood up and moved my throbbing cock to her labia, where she grabbed it and pulled me to her. I hesitated at the entrance, feeling the purple head of my cock pushing against the entrance to heaven. She was impatient and scooted her hips toward me and bucked into me, pushing my dick into her.

She gasped out, "Come ON! Fuck me! Fuck me NOW!"

With that encouragement, I began a heavy thrusting motion into her as she bucked her hips into me and clutched my ass with both hands, pulling me deep into her.

"Oh, yeah! That's it! Harder, Dirk! God damn it, harder!"

She was pretty wound up. I fucked her hard as we slid around on the feed sacks, our sweat acting like grease on the slick sacks. After a few minutes of frenzied fucking, she cried out, "My ass! Stick it in my ass!"

I fumbled around and found the jar of Vaseline, then popped the top. Sticking a finger into the jar, I came up with a gob and smeared it on her asshole, then worked it in with my finger as she moaned. I pulled my cock out of her pussy and decided it was slick enough, then with her hand guiding it, pushed into down a little to her ass.

She about came off the feed sacks as she arched her back and cried out as the intense sensation overwhelmed her as I entered her. I eased in a little at a time as her hands clutched at my ass, then reached up for my head. After a few strokes, I was all the way in as she cried out.

"Oh, God! I've been dreaming about this since last night! I've wanted you in my ass so bad this morning! Fuck me! Fuck me hard! Ohhhhhh! Ahhhhhhh! Play with my clit!"

I pounded into her ass as my balls swelled, filling with cum. I played with her clit and tried to hold on, but the pressure was too much. I cried out.

"I'm coming! Oh, I'm coming!"

She arched her back again.

"Me, too! I'm coming! Oh, shit! Fill my ass with your cum! Oh, damn it! Oh! Owwwww! Keep it up, Dirk! Ahhhhhh! Play with my boobs!"

My cock unleashed several spasms of hot cum into her ass, as she scrambled to keep on top of the slippery sacks while I rammed into her. With both hands, I squeezed her boobs and tweaked the nipples. Her moaning and groaning were constant, and her words were happy gibberish.

I slowed down and then stopped. Her face was a mask of sweat, her eyes tightly closed and her lower lip between her teeth. Her hands were clenched in my hair. Her eyes finally opened, and with my dick still in her ass, she pulled my mouth to hers and started a deep, passionate kiss. After a long while, she released me, and we stared into each other's eyes as our hearts pounded together and our ragged breath rasped heavily. I stroked her wet hair and then ran my hand across her cheeks.

After a few minutes, I straightened up and stood before her. I looked around for a towel, and was able to reach one. I eased back, and my dick came out of her ass in a flood of cum that dripped out of her onto the feed sack. I was the first to speak.

"That was the right decision, to stay at the barn. Pretty fucking hot!"

She grinned at me, still out of breath. "Still want me to suck your dick?"

"Maybe later, thanks."

She reached up and caressed my cheek. "Thanks for doing me. I've been crazy for it since the middle of the night."

"You've surely taken to anal sex."

She laughed. "No shit! It's my new obsession!"

I looked around. "I suppose we should clean up."

"Yeah, give me that towel. I'm leaking like a faucet." She wiped her ass and sat up, then stood shakily.

"Shit, I'm all wobbly."

I held her steady. "How's your ass?"

She grimaced. "Kind of sore, I guess that's to be expected after two sessions like that close to each other. It's okay."

Darla had really enjoyed anal sex, and I had a feeling we would be doing it again in the future. We cleaned up and said goodbye for the weekend. I headed back to town happily tired and sexually satisfied.

The Relationship Matures

Time passed, and I enjoyed seeing Darla about once a month. She would usually call when she got horny and ask me to come over, occasionally coming to my house instead. I helped her with feed runs several more times, each time with her wanting me to finger her on the drive back. She loved the kinkiness of that, and I enjoyed it, too. I got better at keeping the truck on the road during those sessions.

We became friends, and I helped her with farm chores when she asked me to. I even drove her to Texas a few times for horse events, once staying the night in a motel together. I'm sure we kept the neighbors awake with our boisterous activity. I took her to Air Force social events as arm candy a couple of times. She liked hanging out with the men more than the women and got noticed for her rough manner of speaking and sexual comments. I'm sure the officer's wives were outraged, but they needed shaking up now and then. She had me come to a few events with her horsey folks, not that she was close with any of them.

I encouraged Darla to date other men, which she did every now and then. She would tell me about how it went, especially the sex part. There was always sex. She liked to get laid. I liked to see other women, and we both understood that while we enjoyed our sexual experiences and liked being friends, we were not beholden to one another and were free to have a good time with whomever we liked. She still did not want a man hanging around all the time. We enjoyed our time together and I wondered how long it would last.

But I was in the military, and when we started to get involved with Desert Sheild and then Desert Storm late in 1990, I had to deploy to the desert for a month, then got stuck over there for five months during the war. Darla gave me a memorable send-off the night before, and my knees were weak when I boarded the airplane, totally fucked out. It was awesome. I wrote to her saying I got stuck over there for a long time, and I hadn't abandoned her. She wrote back once to say that was fine and she would see me when I got back. When I finally did make it back, she kept me in bed for a couple of days. Another memorable experience.

I got out of the Air Force and drifted without clear goals for a while, selling insurance and working part-time at the Air Force flight simulator as a contract instructor. Darla and I still saw each other, but I was restless and wanted to start flight training. I eventually went to Atlanta to work on my commercial pilot ratings. I came back to the Shreveport area nearly every month for Air Force reserve drill weekends to earn some much-needed money working at the flight simulator. I was burning through cash at an alarming rate with my flight training and earning nothing back. Since I lived in Atlanta now, I no longer had a house in Shreveport, so I usually stayed with Ronni in my old room and partied with her on Friday nights, then would call Darla or another friend on Saturday or Sunday evenings and then head back to training on Monday. Sometimes I'd stay with Darla all weekend. It varied.

This particular weekend Ronni had company, so my old room at her house was occupied, and with the price of hotels, it would nearly negate the money I earned. I called around and got a hold of Darla, explained the situation, and asked if I could stay at her place.

"Sure, Dirk, that would be fine. I have a date planned for Friday, but I'll cancel it."

I didn't want her to do that, she didn't get out very much. "That's okay, Darla. Don't cancel your date on my account. I'll find somewhere else to stay."

She thought for a moment. "What time would you get in on Friday?"

It was my turn to think. "I'm flying in the morning, so about 8 or 9 pm."

"Hell, I'll still be out. Come on and stay at my house. Park your car in the garage. The spare bedroom will be set up for you. You won't bother me at all, and we'll visit as usual on Saturday."

"Thanks, I appreciate it. See you late Friday or Saturday."

Friday at Darla's

After flying on Friday morning, I drove through the dreary December day for the usual 10 hours until I got to Darla's farm. It was dark and rainy for the last few hours of the drive, and I was glad to pull in. Her truck was gone as expected, and I put the car away in the garage. Inside, she had left clean towels on the bed in the spare bedroom, so I used the guest bathroom and took a quick shower.

I was beat from the long day, so I went straight to bed. After reading for a while, I turned out my light and was just getting off to sleep when I heard Darla's truck pull in. I heard another car as well. She must have brought the date home. I heard voices as they came in, then went to sleep, hoping they would have a good visit.

Later, I was awakened by the unmistakable sound of sex. Darla was crying out passionately, so I hoped the date was ringing her bell. I smiled to myself. She needed to get out more, and I was glad she found a guy to screw her when I was not there.

After a short time of dozing back off, I heard a car door shutting, and the sound of it backing down the driveway and driving off. I then heard sounds in the bathroom. I thought to myself he did not stay long after sex, did she throw him out? I'd find out in the morning.

A few minutes later, I heard my door open and then I felt the sheets lift as Darla climbed into bed with me, naked as she usually was when she went to bed. She snuggled up into me, and I leaned over and kissed her as I put my arm around her.

"Hey, pretty lady."

"Hi. How was your drive?"

"Long and full of potholes. It sounded like your date left early."

She laughed as she pushed my tee shirt up and started caressing my chest. "Yeah, he was done pretty quickly. He said something about having to work in the morning, he was out the door five minutes after he came. I think he was embarrassed."

"What happened?"

"Well, I met him for dinner, then we went to my bar where I play pool all the time. I even wore a dress and makeup and all that shit."

"Wow, I'd love to see you in a dress with makeup on."

"If you ever took me anywhere nice, you might see that. Anyway, we had a good time playing pool and joking around, and he seemed nice. I could tell he wanted to fuck me really bad, so I thought what the hell. I need to find someone close by for when I get horny since you are in Atlanta now, so I brought him here to fuck him and see how he did. After hanging out in the living room for a while, I practically had to drag him to the bedroom. We got undressed, then he played with my boobs for about a minute and tried fingering me for less than that, then was ready to get on me. He wasn't really hard yet, so I blew him for a minute, and then he almost came when he was putting his condom on."

"Sounds like he was nervous around you."

"Could be. Anyways, he finally gets on me, and I'm not wet at all since he didn't do hardly any foreplay, so I put some Vaseline on his condom covered dick to make things easier on us both. Some of those things are bone dry. He finally got it in and I could tell he was really excited, so I thought 'Oh boy, this is gonna be over fast.' I was just gonna lay there and let him get his rocks off, but then I thought he really is a nice guy, just super horny and nervous, so I'll be nice and act like he is doing a great job. As he started pumping me, I pretended to be really horny and started making noises like he is the best lover ever, and I pushed up into him like he had me ready to come."

"I heard you; it sounded convincing."

She moved her hand from my chest and was now rubbing my bare thigh. "Good, that's what I was going for. So, he pumps me for about 30 seconds and comes in a blaze of glory, making lots of noise. He stops and pulls out with me looking at him like, 'What the fuck was that?' so I told him that it was great, and we should rest up and do it again. I figured if he rested up and had already come once, he would last longer and maybe do some better foreplay."

"Makes sense, that was very nice of you."

"Hey, I can be nice when I want to. I was trying to make him feel better since he was so nervous. He's a nice guy and I might want to see him again. He gets up and goes into the bathroom, to pull his condom off, I guess. He comes back, puts his clothes on, and says he has to go. Thanks for a nice evening. And he left me laying on the bed naked."

"And unfulfilled."

"No shit. I got up to pee and wipe off and saw his condom in my trash can. That's just rude."

I had to laugh. "I didn't know there was a protocol for condom disposal."

"Well, there should be. He ought to take it with him."

I was stroking her ass as she talked. "So here you are in bed with me, naked."

She laughed. "I'm always naked in bed, don't get a big head. I do have a favor to ask, though."

I could see it coming. "And what might that be?"

She reached a hand into my underwear and put her fist around my cock, and grinned. "Since I am so horny, how about you give me some head until I come which won't take long, then you can fuck me up the ass real quick. Tomorrow we'll take a nice long time, but I want it bad right now."

"Aw jeez, Darla. I've got to get up early to go to work. And I don't think I want to have my face in a pussy that a guy fucked less than an hour ago."

"You're being a wuss. I made him use a condom, so there's no cum inside me. And I washed my pussy off with that soap you like the smell of and put a dab of perfume on my clit."

I was being persuaded. "You do smell nice."

"It's settled, then. C'mon fuck buddy! Take care of your horny friend!" She started stroking my dick. "Ooooh, someone's getting stiff!"

My dick had been getting hard since she had started this conversation. "Since you asked so nice ..."

"There you go!" She rolled onto her back and spread her legs. "C'mon! Get your tongue down here and get busy!"

I was holding out. "How about you give me some deep throat first, to get me in the mood?"

"Damn it! I never should have started that with you. Okay."

She sat up, then bent over and swallowed my cock without hesitation, taking me deep into her throat.

I closed my eyes and groaned. "Damn! That feels great!"

She rose up and looked at me. "There better be some damned good pussy licking after this! I'm horny as shit!"

I smiled. "Not to worry, darlin'. You'll get yours."

After a few minutes of fantastic deep throat action, Darla rose up and said, "Let's go to my bed. I have the Vaseline and washcloths ready."

"I'll follow you."

We changed venues to her bedroom, and after she spread her legs for me while laying on her back, I dove face first into her pussy, admiring the scents and aromas of a fresh cunt. I tried not to think that bachelor number one had fucked this pussy less than an hour ago. I was a little weirded out even though she had assured me he had used a condom. I could smell the perfume she had applied and imagined myself in untouched territory.

Darla bucked and squirmed as I pushed my tongue into her pussy. I went north to say hello to the clit and then back south along the lips to delve into the vaginal vault. As I curled my tongue into her G spot, she exclaimed loudly.

"Oh! Shit! That's the spot! Lick it hard! Ohhhhh!"

I went back up to tickle the clit, prolonging the run-up to her climax.

"Ahhh! Go back inside! Oh, damn, that feels good!"

I kept my attentions on her clit and the inside of her labia, on purpose.

"Damn! C'mon, keep doing it deep! You're teasing me, you fucker!"

I gave her hole and G spot some love, then went back to the clit.

"Quit teasing me and go deeper! Damn it! Come on!"

Since she had asked so nicely, I went back to the hole and tickled the G spot.

"Oh, yeah! Come on! More of that! Stick it in deeper!"

I gave her some hard licks on the G spot, then went to the clit.

"Oh! Shit! Put your cock in my ass! I want to come with you in my ass!"

I rolled her over so she was on her hands and knees, then got a glob of Vaseline from the jar and pushed my cock into her ass with no workup. From experience, I knew she could take the full length of my cock all at once.

"Ahhhh! Oh, yeah! Give my ass a good fucking!"

I started in on her at a good rate and depth, knowing she would ask for it even harder in a few minutes. I didn't have long to wait.

After only a minute, she gasped, "Harder! Harder!"

I increased the pounding of my cock into her, giving it to her pretty hard. Then she had a request.

"Finger me! Finger my spot deep in my pussy!"

That presented a problem. There was no good way to put my finger into her at this angle. "I'll have to roll you on your side."

"Do it! I want to come, finger me!"

I rolled her onto her left side, then straddled her left leg. I lifted her right leg up to my shoulder, so she was 90 degrees sideways to me. I reached down and my finger was still at the wrong angle. I could use my thumb, I guess. I reached for her mouth. "Suck on my thumb and get it wet."

While I continued to pound away, she gave my thumb some treatment like it was a dick, rolling her tongue around it and sucking on it. That was pretty erotic, I'd have to remember that one. I then took the wet thumb and put it into her pussy, turning my hand so the thumb could rub the G spot. I had to reach in pretty far to do that, but found the spot as evidenced by her crying out.

"Oh! Yeah, that's it! Oh, yeah! Ahhhhhh!"

I pounded her asshole even harder while she tried to keep her leg up on my shoulder. My index finger had nothing to do, so I tried to tickle the clit at the same time my thumb was working her G spot. I had a free hand, so I reached around for her boobs and squeezed a nipple, figuring that the combination of all that would send her over the edge. It did.

She screamed, "Ahhhhhhhh! Oh, shit! Oh! Oh! Oh, God! Shit, shit, shit! Owwwwww!"

I felt her body shudder as a wave of orgasm went through her. My balls had loaded up, and I sent a load of hot cum deep into her asshole, with me groaning loudly. I slowed down, then stopped with my dick in her ass. I pulled my thumb out and pressed on her clit as she lay moaning and panting. I moved off her left leg and swung her it over my head so I was now between her legs facing her like the missionary position, managing to keep my dick inside her ass.

Her eyes had been shut, now she opened them and grinned at me. "Even when Rod was fucking me earlier, I was thinking about you here in the next room and you doing that to me! That was great, you putting your thumb in and rubbing my spot!"

"I was glad to be here for you. Is the guy's name Rod?"

"Yeah. Oh! He does the same thing you used to do before you retired."

"Rod is a boom operator?"

"Yeah, in the reserves. That's what he told me anyway."

I thought for a minute. It couldn't be. "Rod Johnston? Medium height, black hair combed back, black mustache?"

"That's him. You know him?"

I phrased my answer carefully. "Yes, I do. I've seen him at the simulator facility. He and I escorted a group of four ladies to the reserve squadron Christmas Party last year. I mean, I don't know him very well."

She shook her head. "Oh, wow. Shall I tell him I know you?"

"Well, honey, since we are laying here with my dick still up your ass, I think saying that you know me is a bit of an understatement."

Her eyes grew wide. "Oh, shit! I've fucked two guys that know each other on the same night! Oh, God! I'm a slut!"

I had to laugh at her. "I'd say you are a horny little shit who just did not get enough satisfaction the first round and was lucky to have your buddy in reserve."

She shook her head again. "Still sounds slutty to me. Are you ever going to pull your dick out of my ass?"

"I kind of like it in there." But I pulled out as she held a cloth under the anus to catch the cum that was dripping out. She stemmed the flood of cum and went trotting to the bathroom. When she came out, I went in and gave my cock a thorough wash, then rejoined her in bed.

I was greeted by a fierce look and a punch in the shoulder.

"Ow! What's that for?"

She was laughing now. "That's for teasing me when I was ready to come, asshole! You made me wait and my frigging head was about to explode, I was so horny!"

I was unapologetic. "Hey, you seemed to like it."

She pulled me in for a kiss. "I did, but you were still an asshole."

"Your asshole seemed like it enjoyed it."

She sighed as she stroked my hair. "I did, and I blame you for getting me started on it so long ago now."

"As I recall from distant memory, you wanted to try it."

"That could be. Or maybe you forced me down and ass raped me."

I snorted in derision.

She looked at me. "How's your back after that long drive?"

I have recurring back pain from an injury while wearing a heavy parachute when I was first in the aircrew business, and then sleeping on a cot for five months during the Gulf War did it no good. "It's kind of tired, but you helped loosen it up."

"I bet I did. Roll over, and I'll massage your back."

I did, but then she changed her mind,

"On second thought, let's go back to the guest room, that way you can go right to sleep after I massage you. We're on different schedules tomorrow, so I'll sleep in here."

We trooped back into the guest room, and still naked, she straddled my hips with me face down and started massaging me.

"That feels nice."

She continued to rub me and started planning our Saturday. "I'm working from noon to six tomorrow to pick up some overtime. What do you want to do about dinner? Pick something up and fix it here, or get takeout, or go out to eat?"

I thought for a minute. "I think go out to eat, but I don't have a lot of extra cash."

"No problem, I'll treat. You've certainly bought me plenty of meals over the years. Where do you want to go?"

"My first choice is always Trejo's for Mexican."

She laughed. "I knew you would say that. I'll come there straight from work. How about 6:30?"

"That's good. I'll be done earlier than that, but I'll hang out at work and surf the Internet on a student computer."

She went from rubbing my lower back to gently caressing me. That always made me sleepy.

After a nice interval, she climbed off. "You got an alarm set?"

I murmured sleepily, "Yes, 0630."

She closed the door on the way out. "See you tomorrow."

I went to sleep almost at once. In the early morning hours, I felt her climb back into my bed. I put my arm around her as she threw a leg over me and hugged me close. This was very unlike normal Darla behavior, she usually did not anyone to touch her while she slept. We did not say a word and soon were both back asleep.

When the alarm went off, I gently disengaged her and shut the damned thing off. I climbed out of bed and got my work clothes out of the closet. I kept some clothes there as spares that I used during my visits. I got out a dress shirt with a tie, slacks, and loafers with socks. Taking all that into the guest bath, I shaved and dressed quietly so she would not be disturbed. Deciding to pick up coffee and something to eat near the base, I headed out in the winter darkness.

At the simulator, I greeted one of the full-time instructors. "How did you get stuck with the weekend?"

He grumbled, "The reserves asked for an extra session, so I got tagged. How was your night?"

I smiled. Well, I got a great blow job, fucked my girlfriend in the ass, and then got massaged to sleep. I'd better not say any of that.

"Pretty good, but I hated to hear the alarm this morning. Whom have we got for students?"

He looked at the schedule. "I've got Adams, and you have Johnston."

I almost spilled my coffee. "Rod Johnston?"

"Yeah. They should be here any time. See you downstairs."

I had to play this very straight. I went downstairs and found Rod at one of the student computers, logging in. "Hi, Rod. Good morning."

He looked up. "Hello, sir. I'm getting logged in to the learning system."

"Call me Dirk, I'm retired now. Let me know when you get your first lesson done, then we have a simulator session at 1030 and another at 1330. "

"Yes, sir... I mean Dirk." He smiled. Maybe he was a nice guy. Would he be good for Darla?

I led Rod through the simulator and learning sessions in a professional manner, but my mind kept wandering. I wonder what his reaction would be if he found out I had fucked Darla an hour after he did? I shook that off, too bizarre to think about. I wondered what Darla's reaction would be when I told her who my student was.

Date Night

I got done with Rod at about 1600, then caught up on the internet while waiting to meet Darla. I was in position at my favorite restaurant a few minutes early when I saw her truck pull in. I walked over to meet her, and when she climbed out, I was stunned. She was wearing a nice dress, had put on makeup, was wearing a necklace and nice shoes.

I said, "Wow, Darla! You look great!"

She smiled shyly. "I wanted to look nice for you tonight after you said you wanted to see me in a dress. We've been dating a long time, and I felt like I should do it for you to show you how much I appreciate all you do for me."

"I appreciate it, thanks!" I gave her a hug and a kiss, which she returned hungrily. We stood in the dark parking lot kissing for at least a long minute.

I pulled back and smiled. "Let's get in out of the cold."

She held my hand as we entered the restaurant. After getting seated and ordering a large margarita, she told me about her day at the hospital. When she got done, we ordered and then I decided to tell her about my day.

"Would you like to guess who my student was today?"

She shrugged. "I have no idea."

"Staff Sergeant Rod Johnston."

Her eyes opened wide. "Are you shitting me?"

"Nope."

She covered her face with her hands. "Oh, God. I don't know whether to laugh or scream!"

I just looked at her. She finally looked at me.

"Did you talk about me?"

I said, "Nope. I acted like I had no idea that you two had dated and played it cool."

She shook her head. "I had no idea that this would happen. What should I do?"

"There's no reason to do anything. It's just a coincidence."

She thought for a moment. "What happens if you see him again?"

I explained, "I have him again all day tomorrow."

She started giggling and could not stop for several minutes. Then she gasped out, "Maybe you can give him some pointers!"

I laughed at that, and she relaxed.

We had a nice dinner, then drove separately the 25 minutes or so up to her farm. Taking our coats off after getting inside, she looked at me with a coy smile. She came to me, put her arms around my neck, and gave me a deep kiss while pushing her hips into me. This behavior was very unlike the normal Darla. She usually wasn't affectionate. I supposed it was the dress making her feel all girly.

She smiled at me after the kiss, then leaned in and on her tiptoes, nibbled my ear lobe like she always did when she had something naughty to say. She whispered, "Don't undress me just yet, I just remembered that I've got a fantasy I want to try."

Oh, boy! Darla had some great fantasies. I was immediately intrigued.

"You told me that just in time, I was going to start taking your clothes off. What do you have in mind?"

She giggled. "I'm working up the nerve to tell you. Let's have a drink while I think about how to explain it to you. What goes with the margaritas we had?"

"Hmm. Something clear. Vodka or tequila. Do you have tequila left from when I made margaritas a while back?"

"I'll go and see."

She came back with two healthy drinks. "Tequila and lime juice!" She announced.

I took a sip. "Damn! This ought to remove any inhibitions you or I have."

She tried hers. "Yep, these are plenty strong. Let's drink, talk, and kiss."

I wondered who had taken possession of Darla's body. She wasn't a talker, normally was not affectionate, and usually only kissed while in the throes of passion. I didn't mind but was wondering what was going on.

She sat on my lap on the loveseat, with her legs over to the side. After kicking her shoes off, she nuzzled her face into my neck and sighed with her arms around my neck.

"Mmmm. This is nice. I feel romantic tonight. What's gotten into me?"

I was stroking her legs and ass over her dress. "I don't know, but I like it as long as it doesn't lead to talk about getting married or anything like that."

She laughed into my neck. "Don't worry, I only want you around on my terms. I guess that's pretty selfish after all the time we have been together. How long has it been?"

I handed her the drink and we both took a swallow. "I don't know. We started at least a year before Desert Storm, and that's been over for more than a year. So almost three years? Does that sound right?"

She took a big swallow and handed me the empty glass. "I guess so. We've had some fun and a lot of great sex. What more could a girl want?"

"I can't argue with you there. I've enjoyed our time together."

She gave me a kiss. "You should be enjoying it, fucker. You get laid pretty regularly for not having to make a commitment. I wanted to fuck your brains out the first time I asked you out here. I've trusted you from the start, and let you do things to me nobody else has. Why is that?"

I played with her boobs over the top of the dress. "We have a sexual chemistry that is a powerful attraction, it's something to do with the hormones, adrenaline, and pheromones in our bodies. I don't know why you instinctively trust me, though."

She swung her legs to the floor. "One more drink, and then we'll talk fantasies."

I went with her to the kitchen, We were both a little unsteady from the big shot of tequila. I said, "Make mine about half of the first one, I have to work tomorrow."

She looked at me, swaying slightly. "All right, be a pussy."

I noticed the message light was blinking on her answering machine and pointed it out to her. "I'll go back to the living room to give you some privacy."

She punched play as I was settling down in the living room. I could hear a man's voice but could not make out the words. I flipped the TV on to give her more privacy and see what was on. Darla came back in with our drinks.

"That was our boy, Rod. He wants to go out again. He left his number. What should I do?"

"If you think you are going to like him, call him back and set up another date. I'll probably leave tomorrow after work, so I'll be out of your hair."

She looked at me. "You don't mind?"

"Hell, no! You need a local dude, and I probably will have to quit coming out here."

She reacted. "What's that about?"

I looked at my watch. "Call Rod back, and I'll tell you about it after."

She went to the kitchen and called Rod. They talked for a few minutes, and then she came back, settling back onto my lap.

"I'm all set to have dinner with Rod tomorrow. How do you think I should handle it?"

"I'd say go out a few times and decide if you like him, then when it feels right, add sex back into the equation. See how that goes."

She gave me a big tequila flavored kiss. "You're the best. I don't think you have a jealous bone in your body."

"I just want what's best for you."

She handed me her empty glass and smiled drunkenly at me. "I'm ready to tell you about my fantasy."

"Go ahead, I'm all ears."

Fantasy Island

She hesitated. "It's kind of role-playing and kind of rough sex. I come home from a date by myself and find a stalker in my driveway. He takes control of me and ties me up. Then he makes me blow him while on my knees in front of him. When I don't do it the way he wants, he grabs my face and holds it while he throat fucks me like it was a pussy, ramming all the way in. Since I've been deep throating you, I don't gag and that makes him furious, so he keeps throat fucking me until he comes, shooting sperm right down my throat, then pushes me down on the floor in disgust and later has rough sex with me."

My eyes were wide. "Wow! That sounds kinky! Where in the world ..."

She laughed nervously. "I've been reading some of those kinky sex novels. That's where I read about something similar, it got me hot thinking about it. Can we do it?"

"Shit, Darla. I don't know. I don't want to hurt you, and this sounds like it is demeaning to a woman, like rape. I guess it could be construed as rape."

"But it isn't rape if we are only role-playing. C'mon, I'm getting hot just talking about it."

The tequila had lowered my inhibitions. "Okay, where do you want me to start?"

"I put a few horse halter ropes in the sunroom, I'll get those so you can tie me up. Then I'll get on my knees in front of you and we'll take it from there."

She got up, so I did, too. She was back in less than 30 seconds with the rope. I tied her hands behind her and then roped her ankles together, and then lowered her gently to her knees.

She looked pretty helpless. "Do you want a pillow for your knees?"

She shook her head no. "In the fantasy, I struggle to keep my balance on my bare knees, still wearing my dress from my date."

"I'm going to take my slacks off and hang them up, I want to wear them again tomorrow."

She smiled nervously. "I'm not going anywhere. When you come back in, be in the role of the stalker. Maybe I jilted you or something and you're getting revenge."

"Okay, but if you get scared or want me to stop, just pull your head back from me real hard. If you have a dick in your mouth and hands tied you can't talk, so I don't know of another way."

She nodded. "Good idea. Make it scary!"

I went to the guest bedroom and hung my slacks up, then pulled my work shirt off and put on a tee shirt, with no pants, only my underwear. I then grabbed a tie to help the role-playing, then went to the coat closet and rummaged around until I found a cold weather ski mask that I used outside during winters. I was ready. I knew she was nervously waiting, hearing me walking around. The tequila had loosened me up.

I walked into the living room. She looked at me in the ski mask, and her eyes opened wide. She was balancing on her knees, shaking a little. I went right into it.

In a rough and husky voice, I said, "Close your eyes, bitch! If you see me, I'll have to make sure you don't tell anyone."

She jumped. "Okay! They're closed."

I wrapped my tie around her eyes, blindfolding her.

"All right, you stuck-up little bitch! You thought you could ignore me, did you? I'm gonna put you in your place. Came home all dressed up, did you? Been on a date? Did you prick tease another man tonight?"

She stammered, "No, there must be some mistake..."

"Shut up, bitch!"

I was standing over her. I pulled her head forward roughly until her face was against my underwear. I'm sure my boner was easily felt.

"Feel that, bitch? That's my cock, just as stiff as it was when you turned me down. Put your mouth on it. Then pull my shorts off with your teeth. Too bad you can't use your hands, right?"

She mouthed my dick through the shorts, then started trying to get the waistband of the shorts in her teeth, stretching and craning.

She cried out, "It's too hard, I can't do it!"

I pulled the waistband down so she could get it.

"Here, damn it! Pull the shorts down, then suck my cock!"

My dick plopped out of the shorts, and as she tried to get it in her mouth, I slapped it against her cheek a few times, then pulled her to it.

"All right, no more excuses. Start sucking, and it better be good!"

She went to work, bobbing her head on my rock hard dick, running her tongue around the shaft and rimming the glans. She alternated that with deep throating me, and it felt great. I let her do that for a few minutes, then went into my act.

"That's not good enough, damn it! Hold your ass still, I'm going to hold your head and show you how to do it! You'd better not bite me! Get your mouth open. Wider!"

I held her head and started pumping into her wide open mouth, going a little deeper each time until I could feel the head of my dick going into her throat. I started thrusting harder and harder, with my balls slapping her under her chin on each push. It felt fantastic.

It was time for more drama. "Damn it, you ought to be gagging by now! You little bitch, I'm going to come right down your throat! Maybe that will make you gag!"

She was not pulling back at all, so I ramped up the motion and after a minute of fantastic feeling, I was feeling my balls fill up. I was going to come any second, and she said to do it right down her throat. Here goes!

"All right, you cunt! Here it is! Ahhhhhh!"

I let loose a torrent of cum down her throat as I held her head into me. She started a muffled groaning and moaning but did not pull back, so I emptied my dick into her and then pulled out.

"All right, that was good enough. You just wait here, and I'll be back later to fuck you."

To complete the fantasy, I pulled her to the floor and left her panting, with saliva and a little cum drooling out of her mouth. I walked away and left her bound hand and foot. She was immobilized.

A minute or so later, I walked back in.

"It's me being Dirk again. Are you all right?"

She tried to sit up. "That was fucking amazing. You scared the shit out of me for a few minutes!"

I took off the blindfold.

"Ready to be untied?"

"Yeah! Damn, that was crazy. So fucking kinky! Did you hear me come? I bet my pussy is sopping wet. Damn!"

I untied her, and she sat up, rubbing her wrists.

I was immediately concerned. "Did I hurt your wrists?"

She shook her head, "No, that was just right. Hold me for a minute! I'm still a little scared but in a good way!"

After holding her for a minute, she wanted to get up and use the bathroom, She came back after a few minutes, wearing a long tee shirt, and carrying a bath towel.

"Here, let's sit on this." We sat on the loveseat together. She took my hand and put it on her naked pussy under the tee shirt. "See? I'm still wet even after drying off. Wow! That was incredible. Have you done anything like that before?"

"Nope. First time."

She shook her head. "That is a whole new level of sex play. Damn!"

We curled up together and pulled a blanket over us, watching TV quietly for a while as she calmed down. After a while, she looked at me.

"What's this about you not coming out here anymore?"

I looked into her eyes. "After this next check ride, I hope to be a full-time instructor, flying every day. I won't be able to come out here to work at the simulator because I will be flying a lot. That's my goal, to build flying time and eventually get on with the airlines."

She pondered that. "I guess I knew that was coming. I just wasn't expecting it to happen so soon, or I was hoping it would not happen at all. Will you come out to visit me sometime?"

I stroked her hair. "I hope to. Or you could come to see me."

She leaned into me. "Hmmph. I hope so. I'm gonna miss your regular visits, like when you were away during the war. I don't mind telling you I was lonely for you then."

"I know, honey. I missed you, too. For two people who are not in a serious relationship, we are pretty close."

Darla pulled back and sat up, looking straight into my eyes. "You know I love you, right?"

I leaned over and kissed her. "I know. And I love you, Darla. As a dear and good friend that I'll miss very much."

She leaned back into me. "I just wanted to make sure I told you that in person since I've never said it before but have felt that for a long time. We're fuck buddies that love each other as friends, whatever the fuck that means."

I kissed the top of her head. "We're starting a new category. Lovers, friends, buddies."

She shook her head into my shoulder. "This is going to be fucked up until we get used to it. We'll keep having fun until then. That's all I'm going to say about it."

"Me, too."

We sat in silence for a while, lost in our thoughts and our memories of the crazy times we had. After a long time, I looked at my watch. It was late and I had to work in the morning, then drive ten hours back to Atlanta. That was sounding less and less like a good idea.

"Hey, honey. Let's go to bed."

"Good idea. Can you sleep with me tonight? I want you to."

"Sure thing."

We got ready for bed, and as we got settled, she rolled over to me and put her hand on my dick.

She smiled, "I'll give you some pussy since you have not been in it yet this weekend. You don't need to do a lot of foreplay, just get hard and get on me."

"That's very nice of you."

She pumped my dick while grinning at me. "Hey, I told you I can be nice. See if I'm wet enough. I'll put some Vaseline in there if we need it."

I slipped a finger in her and gave her G spot a little tickle.

"Feels good to me."

She rolled on her back and spread her legs. "Stop that! You're good and hard. It must be tough to never get any sex, you horny poor thing, springing a boner with 30 seconds of cock rubbing. Fuck me now before I change my mind."

I was laughing as I rolled on top of her. "Yeah, if only I could have sex every now and then. I'm neglected."

She laughed, too. I entered her, and as I slid my cock all the way in, stopped and savored the feeling for a moment. She noticed.

"What's wrong, why did you stop?"

I laughed. "I'm enjoying the moment. You have the sweetest damn pussy, and I'm relishing being in you."

"You always say something nice about it, is it really good? Be honest with me."

I looked her in the eyes. "Darla, honey. This is absolute USA Prime Grade A pussy. It's just the right tightness, it's warm and wet, just deep enough, has a cute, shaved exterior with lips that are meaty enough, and smells and tastes like a little bit of heaven."

She giggled. "Oh, my! I've never heard you talk like this."

"Honey, if word gets out about this pussy, you'll have men lined up from here to the highway with flowers in their hands and their tongues hanging out."

"You really know how to sweet talk a girl. Now, c'mon and get busy."

We settled into a nice relaxing fuck, taking our time, and relishing the feeling of each other. I played with her boobs, and she caressed my chest, back, and ass. After several enjoyable minutes, I picked up the pace and ejaculated into her with a loud groan. She was stroking my hair.

"There you go. Now you can get to sleep right away. Roll over, and I'll scratch your back."

I rolled over. "Wow, royal treatment tonight."

She started scratching my back. "I'm feeling mushy tonight, don't piss me off. Did you set an alarm?"

"Yes, Ma'am."

I dozed off almost right away, then rolled toward her. She snuggled up into me with an arm across my chest and a leg thrown over mine. After a minute, I was almost asleep but felt her gently kiss my cheek and whisper, "I love you, Dirk."

I whispered back, "I love you, Darla."

Goodbye

It was in the early morning hours when something woke me. I looked at my watch, it was not time for the alarm yet. I felt something and then noticed Darla had rolled over all the way to her side of the bed, facing away from me with her shoulders convulsing as she wept silently. I rolled over to her and put my arms around her. She turned over to me and sobbed quietly as I held her, with tears streaming down her cheeks. I had never seen her cry. Stroking her hair and talking softly to comfort her, she slowed down and then stopped, sniffling. I kissed her eyelids, cheeks, and then her lips, tasting salty tears and trying to soothe her as she buried her face in my neck.

A few minutes later she pulled back from me, and without a word, pushed me onto my back and laid on top of me, her legs straddling mine. We lay like that without moving for several minutes, then she reached down to put her hand on my dick and guided me to her labia. I started getting hard at once, and she pulled me gently into her while she lay on top of me. I began thrusting slowly and gently into her as she lay with her eyes closed as I ran my hands up and down her back and ass.

Then she sat up, drew her legs up, and was riding my dick sitting up while bracing herself with her hands on my shoulders. She started crying again, with her hips moving, and me pumping up into her while tears rolled down her cheeks. After a few minutes, she stopped crying and collapsed on top of me, then said, "Roll me over. Get on top of me."

I rolled us over, with my cock still in her. I was getting harder and harder, and soon was deep inside her. Her hips pushed into me as I pumped her, and after about five minutes of gentle lovemaking, her textures changed, her breath became rapid and ragged, and soft moans started from her mouth. I took my cues from her and started pushing deeper and faster.

She whispered into my ear, "Harder, Dirk."

I pushed in deeper and soon was hearing that fantastic slapping sound of flesh against flesh, the sweet sound of hot sex. After a minute of that, she moaned deeply and made soft mewing noises as a gentle orgasm swept over her. I felt a gentle shudder from her and she was done. I was right behind her as my balls sent a stream of hot cum deep within her. I stopped and stayed in her as we lay together, enjoying the afterglow.

Her eyes finally opened, and she looked deep into mine. She rose up and kissed me sweetly, her lips still salty from tears.

Then, the tender interlude was over. Her face changed from a soft look of gentle intimacy to one of expressionlessness. At that moment, she reverted to the lady with the rough persona and gave me a hard squeeze on my ass cheek then said, "If you'll get off me, I'll wash up and make you some coffee before you go."

I had to smile, that was classic Darla. "You got it."

After hitting the shower in the guest bathroom, getting dressed, and packing up most of my things, I hesitated, then got all my spare clothes out of the closet and looked around for any of my personal stuff that had accumulated here over the years. There were more than a few items. I carried my bag out to the car and came back in.

Darla was standing at the kitchen island, holding out a paper cup of coffee with cream, just the way I liked it. I sipped it silently, feeling like whatever I said would not be the right thing. She broke the ice.

"Have a good day at work and a safe trip home. Don't say anything to Rod, please. I'll see him tonight, and I'm still trying to work out how to approach that."

"Let me know how that works out. I'll probably be back here one more time, but I'm not sure when. Maybe January or February. "

In a moment of tenderness, she came to me and put her arms around me, laying her head on my shoulder. "You're always welcome here, Dirk. Anytime you want, please stop by. No strings, no long-term anything." She moved her head to look at me and put a hand on my cheek. "Just love from your old friend. Goodbye, Dirk. It's been great."

I shook my head. "I'm going to say I'll see you later, not goodbye."

She smiled bravely, on the verge of tears again. "See you later, then."

Getting into my car, I shivered in the damp, dark Louisiana cold. The sun was just coming up in the east. Backing out, I didn't look back to see if she was watching out the window.

I made it through work that day like an automaton, treating Rod like a nameless entity. Professional, with no fluff or emotion. I signed his training record and shook his hand, wishing him the best. I really wanted to say, "Take good care of my friend, or I'll hunt you down and break both your legs." But I didn't.

I shook hands with my colleagues, said I would see them on the next trip, and was soon eastbound on I-20, heading to Atlanta and the next phase of my new career.

That was my last trip to Shreveport. I never saw Darla again.

Don't miss out!

Visit the website below and you can sign up to receive emails whenever Dirk Caldwell publishes a new book. There's no charge and no obligation.

https://books2read.com/r/B-A-UHDZ-JPBOC

BOOKS 2 READ

Connecting independent readers to independent writers.

Did you love *Back to the Farm with Darla - A Sexy Sequel*? Then you should read *Flight Attendants want Love: Flying High with Jessica*[1] by Dirk Caldwell!

Dirk's novels always weave a romantic story amid the sex scenes. Both Men and Women will enjoy this book with plentiful details about airline crew romances.

Airline pilot Dirk meets flight attendant Jessica, and their initial sexy encounter grows into a relationship that spans decades, through good times and bad. The author incorporates exquisite details, bringing the reader into the bedroom with the couple to feel the heat. Fly along with Dirk and Jessica as they travel the world of sensuality.

1. https://books2read.com/u/brBaPW

2. https://books2read.com/u/brBaPW

About the Author

Dirk Caldwell is the pen name of the author of an erotic book series. Dirk embodies the life experiences of the author as an Air Force veteran and commercial airline pilot. Most of the content is true and relates to the author's experiences. It's up to the reader to decide what is fiction and what is true life.

Milton Keynes UK
Ingram Content Group UK Ltd.
UKHW020723290923
429627UK00015B/697